THIS BOOK
BELONGS TO

_____

THE OTHER SIDE

A. M. MARCUS

Adam was a busy boy. He cheerfully helped his mother around the house by doing chores and taking care of his father, who was sick.

4

In the evening, when his work was finished, he liked to spend time outside relaxing.

One evening, as the sun dropped lower, Adam hurried to his favorite place on the hill so that he could enjoy a great view of the sunset.

9

Once there, he noticed a tree had been cut down and he could now see a house on a hill on the other side of the valley.

As the sun set, Adam noticed an amazing light on the house. The windows of the house began to glow very bright. Adam was sure the house must have golden windows. It was so beautiful that Adam wished that the windows on his house were golden, too.

11

12

After a bit, the sun disappeared, the first stars began to twinkle, and the people who lived there closed the blinds. Once that happened, the house resembled his own quite a bit.

13

One day, Adam's mother told him that she was so thankful for all his help, that she wanted him to take the whole day to himself...to explore and have fun and to not worry about doing any chores.

Adam was so excited! As he left, he grabbed a snack and told his mother good-bye.

She nodded and told him, "I hope your day is adventuresome and full of discovery."

As he headed down the path, Adam knew exactly where he was going and what he wanted to do. He would find the house with the windows of gold.

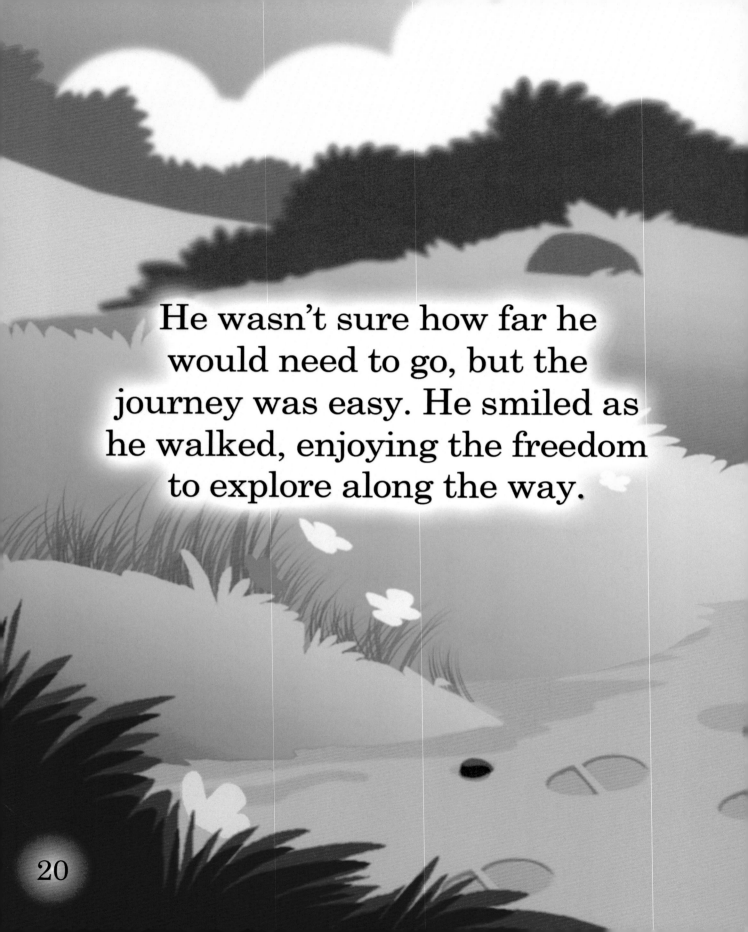

He wasn't sure how far he would need to go, but the journey was easy. He smiled as he walked, enjoying the freedom to explore along the way.

Eventually, he stopped at a pond to eat his snack, which he shared with a few geese that gathered around.

23

Awhile later, he found himself at the bottom of the hill that had the house with the golden windows. He was so excited, he began to run.

When he got to the house, however, his heart sank. The house didn't have windows made of gold. They were just normal glass windows. In fact, one pane even had a crack in it. Was he at the right house, he wondered?

Disappointed, he turned to leave. As he did, a woman stepped outside and said, "Hello, are you lost? Can I help you?"

Adam shook his head and replied, "No, I thought I saw a house across the valley with golden windows. I wanted to see them up close, but now that I'm here, I realize I was wrong."

The woman chuckled and said "No, I'm sorry, we don't have golden windows. We are simple country people with nothing fancy. However, I just baked some cookies. Would you like to come in and have some? I also have a daughter about your age. Perhaps you'd like to meet her."

Adam nodded and followed the woman to her kitchen. She gave him a plate of warm cookies and a glass of cold milk.

As he ate, she called up the stairs to her daughter.

A girl about his age walked into the kitchen as Adam munched on his cookies.

"Hey, I'm Mary. What's your name?" she greeted. "Adamth," he sputtered, with his mouth full. Mary giggled.

Mary showed Adam around her home. First, they played with some toys she had in her room. Then, she invited Adam to play some video games with her.

They went to the stables as well, and Mary introduced her white horse, which was similar to the black horse that Adam had at home.

It was obvious that Mary and Adam were becoming fast friends.

After a wonderful visit, Adam thanked Mary for the visit and they said good-bye.

A few days later, Mary called to invite him for breakfast the next morning, as she had something else to share with him. Adam eagerly agreed.

The next morning, before breakfast, Mary told Adam she wanted to take him to her favorite place on the edge of the hill to show him something special.

"I love to come here and watch the sunrise," Mary said.

"Across the valley, each morning, I
see a house that has golden windows.
They shine as bright as the sun itself.
I wish I could live there."

Adam looked at her in awe. "You
see golden windows, too? So do I!
That's what I was looking for the
first day I came here. I see them at
sunset, though."

Mary nodded. "See the home over there? The golden windows should appear about right now." Adam looked at the home on the other side.

Just then the sun shone on it and the windows began to glow a beautiful golden color. Adam almost couldn't believe his eyes!

49

"That's my house we're looking at!"
he declared. "But our windows
aren't really gold!"

Mary was shocked and replied, "I guess that when we think things on the other side are better, most of the time we don't really know." Adam nodded at her wise words.

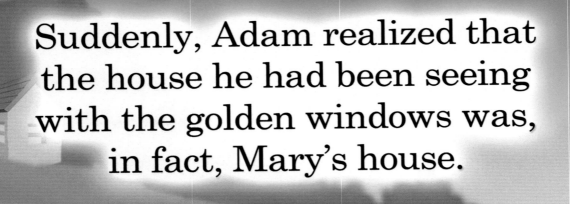

Suddenly, Adam realized that the house he had been seeing with the golden windows was, in fact, Mary's house.

Though they weren't actually golden and were only reflecting the sun, somehow he didn't feel so disappointed. He knew then that his home was just as special as Mary's.

THE END

Don't forget
your FREE GIFT

I remember being your age

I wish that someone had asked me the questions I am about to ask you when I was younger. I know you are very smart and can think for yourself. How would you answer these questions?

• Have you ever seen something that looked amazing from a distance, but when you got close, it did not seem as special?

• Can you think of a time when you changed your point of view, and found that what you are seeing looks quite different?

• Have you ever looked at your life and thought perhaps someone else has it much better? Do you think it is possible that they also think the same when they compare their life to yours?

• When you understand that you don't really know someone else's life, how could you possibly envy them?

I would love to know what you think of my book!
Please send me an email: author@AMMarcus.com
or share your thoughts with the rest of the world on Amazon.

Scan and post a review

A word from me to the grown-ups

I hope this story has helped you start a dialogue with your children about the value of appreciating what they have. Too often we are drawn into the trap of believing that other people's lives are superior to ours, without truly knowing what their true circumstances are. Just as Adam thinks the house on the other side of the valley is better than his, but learns differently, your child will soon discover that more often than not "the grass isn't always greener" on the other side.

I hope I have inspired both you and your children.
If you liked this book, would you consider posting a review?
Your help in spreading the word is greatly appreciated. Reviews from readers like you make a huge difference in helping new readers find children's books with powerful lessons similar to this book.

I would love to hear from you! Please subscribe to my email newsletter following the link on the last page. In the newsletter you will find exciting updates, promotions, and more.

Follow this direct link to post a review

go.ammarcus.com/other-review

Some personal things about me

My favorite fruits: Strawberries & Raspberries

My favorite school subjects: Math & Computers

My favorite hobby: Dancing & Teaching Salsa

My favorite color: Green

My favorite animal: Tiger

My favorite sport: Soccer

My favorite pet: Dogs

Don't forget your
FREE GIFT
on the last page

And a little bit more...

I graduated from the Technion Israel Institute Of Technology with B.Sc. Cum Laude in Computer Engineering. Throughout my studies, I have been teaching and helping children with math and through my work, I have helped them to discover their inner strength and motivation to continue studying and nurturing success in life.

I love the challenge of early education, and especially enjoy working with children with learning difficulties. I have found great satisfaction in helping them conquer their fears and overcome the challenges associated with their education.

I have read dozens of self-improvement books, and have been influenced heavily by them. Through self-reflection, I have found that my great dream was to share that wisdom and my numerous life lessons with people, but especially with kids.
I left my computer engineering career in order to pursue my dream of becoming an author of children's books. Today, I continue to write these books, with the goal of teaching kids basic skills through storytelling. I believe that a good story is an excellent way to communicate ideas to children.

Each and every story is based upon some deep issue, value, or virtue that can potentially make a huge impact on the lives of both you and your children. I have a vast collection of quotes, and usually I base my stories off of quotes I personally find inspiring. The lesson of this book, for example, can be summed up in an inspirational quote by author C.S. Lewis. Turn the page to check the quote.

www.AMMarcus.com

"What you see and what you hear depends a great deal on where you are standing."

-C.S. Lewis, British novelist

More books
by A. M. Marcus

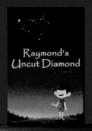

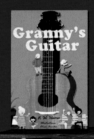

Coming soon!

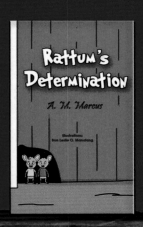

**Don't forget
your FREE GIFT**

Scan to get your FREE GIFT

ammarcus/free-gift

Use the code to get the gift:
994512

Made in the USA
Middletown, DE
01 November 2017